For Rachel

All by Myself
Copyright © 2000 by Ivan Bates
Printed in Hong Kong. All rights reserved.
http://www.harperchildrens.com
Library of Congress catalog card number: 99–71483
Originally published by Oxford University Press,
Great Clarendon Street, Oxford OX2 6DP, England.

1 2 3 4 5 6 7 8 9 10
❖
First HarperCollins Edition

# All by Myself

## Ivan Bates

HarperCollins*Publishers*

Every morning, Maya and her mother had breakfast together. Maya's mother would reach her long trunk high into the branches of a tree and pick the juiciest leaves for them to eat together.

But one morning, just as her mother was about to reach up and pick some leaves for breakfast, Maya said, "I want to do it."

"But you are just
a little elephant,"
said her mother.
"I want to do it,"
said Maya,
"all by myself."
"Very well,"
said her mother.

Maya looked at the tree.
It was very tall. The leaves
seemed very far away.
She thought for a bit.

Then she picked up a
branch that was lying
on the ground, and
stretching up as
high as she could,

### SWISH!

She swished at the
branches above,
trying to knock
the leaves down.
The branches
swayed and shook.

But the leaves did not fall.

An old lion, who was snoozing nearby, came to see what all the swishing was about.

"I can climb the tree with my claws and pick you some leaves, if you like," he growled sleepily.

"No thank you," said Maya politely. "I want to do it, all by myself."

Maya thought some more.
Then she had another idea.

She ran down to the water hole. There
she stretched out her trunk and sucked up
as much water as she could.

When her trunk was
full, she ran back to
the tree, pointed her
trunk, and blew!

*WHOOSH!*

The water whooshed
into the tree, getting
everyone wet. The
branches splashed
and dripped.

But the leaves
did not fall.

A bird who had been sunbathing at
the top of the tree came down to see
what all the whooshing was about.

"What do you think you're doing?"
she squawked, flapping water
off her wings.

When Maya explained,
the bird chirped, "I can fly
to the top of the tree and
pick you some leaves,
if you like."

"No thank you," said Maya.
"I want to do it, all by myself."

Maya looked up at the tree
and thought very hard.

Then she stepped back three
paces, took a deep breath and
charged at the tree, pushing
the trunk as hard as she could.

*BUMP!*

But the tree did not move
and the leaves did not fall.

"My head hurts,"
said Maya sadly.

Suddenly a snake
appeared from
underneath a rock.
"If you like,"
he hissed, "I can
slither up and pick
you some leaves."

"No thank you,"
Maya whispered.
"I want to do it,
all by myself."

But this time Maya had
no ideas. It was such a
tall tree and she was
only a little elephant.
Then a voice she knew
very well said gently,
"I have an idea."

And with that, Maya's mother carefully slipped her long tusks under Maya, and curling her trunk around her little elephant, lifted her high into the branches of the tall tree. Maya stretched out her trunk and picked all the juiciest and greenest leaves she could. All by herself.

Maya was a very
happy little elephant.
And her mother was
a very proud mother.
Together they ate their
breakfast, and Maya
thought it was the very
best breakfast she'd
ever had.

Then together they strolled off across
the plains as the sun rose in the sky.